IKE MORAH

authorHOUSE®

AuthorHouse™
1663 Liberty Drive
Bloomington, IN 47403
www.authorhouse.com
Phone: 1-800-839-8640

Published by AuthorHouse   05/08/2012

ISBN: 978-1-4685-9821-6 (sc)
ISBN: 978-1-4685-9822-3 (e)

Library of Congress Control Number: 2012908308

It was very early one spring morning that it all started. Johnny Cash was his name. Some of his friends, and he had a lot of them too, called him BF Cash—Baby Face Cash. He was one hunk of a man and that is apart from being very handsome. Many members of the opposite sex would simply describe him as being "all that," if you know what I mean.

The early morning dew was still fresh on the grass blades and the flimsier longer ones actually drooped from their weight. Were one to walk through them, one was surely going to wet both his shoes and pants. They were very fresh and he could see a few early birds lapping up those drops. To them it was like honey from the gods. The mist was rather thin and the air crisp though not nippy, and very fresh. The scent of the prairie here was a delicious mixture and blend of wild lavenders and lilacs. This scent alone was enough to make one feel as if he were in heaven.

He had just come out from a roadside motel where he had passed the previous night and he was now on his way to nowhere. He was the Chief Executive officer of a computer microchip company. He was on a month long vacation. He had decided to take a tour of the country, or at least his region without using his car. He believed that paying for transport and hitching hikes might be more fun. Apart from this, he wanted to experience what the poorer folks went through. He was out for a first hand experience of what most people experienced.

For this purpose he had decided to travel very light. He had both a credit card and Automated Transaction Machine card. These came together with a sizable stash of cash. As it was pointed out, he travelled light—really very light. He had a few toiletries, and two changes of clothing all in a near empty travelling bag which was slung over his back.

He stood there and watched more early birds come with each singing happily in full-throated ease. Most of the songs seemed to be in happiness for the arrival of another day. That was part of what he had come out for—to see and experience unpolluted nature at its best. One of the birds actually boldly came very close to where he was. Maybe he was standing there so motionlessly that it had taken him to be one of those strange trees. It was probably more likely going to be a young bird that had just learnt to fly and so had not yet developed that fear for humans. It had fiercely bright blue and red feathers, which made it stand out in that early spring morning. It lapped up a few dewdrops, as if they were actually very delicious, before taking off to a safer distance from him.

The early rays of the sun had shot upwards and across the skies from the east. They came on subdued as if they were too shy to compete with the now fast receding moon. The sun itself was beginning to rear its head from deep down that eastern horizon. It seemed very reluctant at fist, but as time went on it, came up at a much faster pace. That eastern horizon therefore took on a light bronze hue. From the western horizon he could still see those fast receding silvery rays of the moon as it vanished, to reappear once more the next night. Everywhere was beginning to look very bright, as there was not even a single fair-weather cloud in the sky.

The breeze was very mild. It was so mild that even its gusts were barely perceptible at a lazy five miles per hour speed. It was so mild that even those strongest gusts were barely able to stir the dried leaves that were left on the ground from after the last autumn.

Just at that moment, a cockerel from a neighboring farm crowed. He could see it perched on a mound like the wind vane with an ample supply of comb and wattles that quaked. He was actually only exhibiting for a flock of pretty hens that were pecking nearby. Naturally it was always mating season for these cocks and he never failed to notice that. In a flash he was down and about chasing those girls and women. Maybe it was the mild spring weather that was having that effect on that cockerel, maybe it wasn't. It was however also beginning to have the same effect on him.

He was not too sure of where he was, neither was he very sure of where he was headed to. One thing was however sure; he was going to explore the country further and he was in the mood for just that. He still had about twenty-eight working days left for that.

It was at that very moment that he saw the headlights of a car as it came towards him in a distance. It came very slowly. He immediately moved to a more vantage position nearer to the road and began to flag it down. It was time for a hike. He was headed to anywhere in that general direction that the car was travelling. The car further slowed down as it came towards where he was and he was beginning to feel lucky. It slowed down almost to a complete stop right in front of him before it suddenly sped on. That was abnormal, unless someone was only trying to taunt him or maybe the driver was afraid at the last moment. Some will never pick up a total stranger along the road.

What he saw as the car stopped momentarily was however enough to put him on fire. The car was a brand new BMW 7 series and it was one of the latest models. It was a convertible with its roof down. Obviously the occupant was also enjoying the cool early spring morning. Whoever it was must be rich too; after all it is not the average Joe who could afford such a ride. The most important thing about the car was however its driver.

At the very instant that the car had slowed to a near total stop, their eyes had interlocked! He was transfixed by what he beheld and she was probably equally mesmerized by the sight of him. He had never seen a female as beautiful as she was. She was indeed both beautiful and pretty. That was the only way that he could think of her. It was still very early in the morning and she looked rather very fresh with the wind teasing its way through her lovely coiffeurs. He was instantly jealous of the wind. From what he had seen, even Madonna would be very jealous, of not just those coiffeurs, but also of that face. Though he had but seen only very little of her, he knew that she should be well endured.

That small encounter was enough for him to make up his mind, and it was also probably more than enough for her. It must have been what made her drive off like that without thinking, as it seemed. She had however stolen his heart.

Why did she drive off like that without him? Was it to taunt him? He was of course going to find that out for himself. Now his roaming around was going to have a purpose. She was gone as she had come but she had refused to get out of his mind since her presence had seared its way through him. Though it was but a very short encounter, it was more than enough for him. For him the phrase 'love at first sight' had become a reality. It was no longer a theory, neither was it any longer a story or just a saying. It had become a reality and a practical affair of the mind. It had become a concrete reality and an obsession. He immediately began to long for her and so he made up his mind to go after her.

She had come like the wind from nowhere in particular, and like the wind she had gone too, and yet she was still there. He was now resolved on finding her but where to start was going to be a problem. All he knew was that she had driven off in one particular direction, and that was that. He was however going to chase after her in that general direction.

It was like chasing the wind.

This was what made him remember a poetic composition that he had once come across:

Loves Strangest Path

Amuck my feelings flirt and run
With viscera clenched in mild unease;
Calm anticipation my fascination taunts
As floodgates of passion do bang ajar.

Along love's strangest path I stray
Consumed by burning love for you.
Bewitched, my passions quickened stray _
A writhing heart in need of you.

My worldly quest is for thy love to get
You noble art, a natures being,
Lovely and daring you never fret
And time can't molt my love for you.

Sweet and comely I long for you
My emotions with desires enriched;
Unforgettable I long for you—
A miracle or is it a waking trance?

As tranquil dreams like phantoms come
Murmury soft to my lonely heart;
Fragrant and sweet my honeyed love
So vapory and soft you soothe my yearning heart.

(Adapted from the book of poetry: Enchanted Mead, by
Ikechukwu Morah)

This was the poem that came to his mind when he saw her. It only came to reflect what was in his mind at that very moment.

It was at that moment that he remembered the story that was told of the origins of giants in biblical times. It was claimed to have come from the Book of Enoch. The story went to the effect that God had sent some of his angels down to the earth on a mission. When they came down, they discovered that the fair daughters of men in that area were very beautiful. For them to think so meant that these ladies were prettier than those in heaven, obviously prettier than the angels. They therefore decided to abandon their mission and stay on earth to marry those beautiful things. It was their offsprings with these women that became giants.

Johnny did not blame himself for falling in love with that pretty lady at first sight. She was obviously prettier than the ones that those angels met, so who was he not to fall for her.

She had awoken his innermost feelings and she seemed to have conspired with the mild breeze that was now blowing to mess with his feelings. They had struck him blind—blind from what one might call deductive reasoning. They had conspired to make him fall in love in an instant, and he was now blind to every other thing except for her. No wonder it is claimed that 'love is blind.'

His only aim now was to go after her. Like the wind she had come and like the wind she had gone. He however knew that she had gone towards the west and so west it was going to be. He did not know who she was, where she had come from or where she was headed. For now he did not even care as to whether she was married or single. One thing that he now imagined was her sweet huskily feminine voice as she talked to him. It was however only playing out in his mind. Love had stuck him mad with at least partial insanity, if it was insane to fall in love. He was beginning to hear voices in his head.

He could hear her very loudly in his head, not minding the fact that neither of them ever uttered a single word to each other. All that he could remember, this was not imagined, is that she had given him one heck of a wink as she sped off. It was a suggestive and enticing type of wink. It was a wink that was fully pregnant with meanings. It was but a wink, but it spoke volumes, and he knew what it was. She had also probably fallen for him though she was afraid to face it and that was why she drove off. In his minds ears he could hear her very clearly as she spoke:

"Come on my dear, this honey pot is all yours."

"I am on my way." He thought he heard himself reply.

"Try your luck and do not fail me for I am worth it for you."

"Where can I find you?"

"Just try."

"Where should I start?"

"As I had said, just try. Try, try and try again. It is claimed that perseverance overcomes all obstacles and so please try my dearest!"

"How?"

"I don't know. Nothing is easy, at least not as easy as it will ever look. One will always persevere to get to his goal and this pot of honey is not different. The way to the sweetest things in life is never all that easy. Consider the honey. Not minding how sweet it might taste, one would have to brave it through the bees to get to it and it is never easy. What of the rose flower? A rose flower on its own speaks volumes when presented to a lady, but one can never get to it in a rose bush except through the thorns. That is how I am."

"Say no more for I am coming after you."

It was at this very juncture that he came back to his senses. It took the appearance of a young boy, probably a student, on a bike for him to come to an inspiration. The young boy must have been on an early morning errand on an old motorcycle. He flagged the boy down for a lift:

"Where are you headed to sir?" That was how the boy asked the question. He was obviously a well brought up kid.

"Wherever the next city is in that general direction."

"It seems that you are new here. That would be some three hundred miles away. I am only headed for the gas station over there to buy some groceries."

"Is this bike yours?"

"Of course it is."

"What do you do for a living?"

"I am a student. But why do you ask so many questions?"

"I'll tell you in time, but how much do you think that this bike is worth?"

"Mister, you seem to be the inquisitive type."

"I know."

"It's worth maybe around three hundred dollars."

"I guess six hundred if it were still new."

"You happen to be correct, but how did you know that? It was exactly how much my dad paid for it when he bought it for me some five years ago."

"What would you say if I offered you two big ones for it"?

"Two big ones?"

"You heard me right."

"Two thousand dollars to be exact?"

"Yes."

"Then I'll say that it's a deal."

"In that case a deal it is."

Johnny fished out his wallet from his back pocket, riffled through its various compartments and handed the boy two thousand dollars.

"Men you just got yourself a reliable bike." He said as he counted his money happily.

"I hope so."

The boys mind was already on his next project. What Johnny did not know was that there was a bike dealer in the village, and the boy had always had his eyes on one particular bike there, but he could not afford it. It was a Kawasaki Stereo King Fisher bike, and its price tag was one thousand one hundred dollars, and he was headed straight for that dealership.

His eyes were wide open with glee as he handed the particulars over together with the keys and a bill of sale, which he scribbled on a sheet of paper that Johnny had provided.

"Thank you sir." He greeted as he headed back on foot.

"No it's me who should thank you. You might not realize what you have just done for me. It is therefore my duty, and the onus falls on me to thank you."

"Whatever, I accept the thanks even before you say it. And see you next time."

It was not just the boy who was in a hurry. Johnny was in a hurry too. He was already on the bike and he was headed in the general direction of the west as he had planned. His quest was to try and catch up with his physical wind—the apple of his heart. It was a gamble and he was ready to take it, after all life itself was one big gamble. According to the boy, the city was about three hundred miles away and she looked like the type that one could find only in a big city. She was pretty, she was comely and she looked sophisticated, to state the least.

Apart from stopping three times to fill up his tank, it took him the better part of seven hours to get there. It was the capital city of the province and an old city at that, but it was famous for being the melting pot of the different groups as well as characters in the nation. It was one of those cities where night never fell. People milled around by night just as they did at daytime. It was not a particularly modern city but it was built in olden times around where prospectors mined for gold and now it was for diamond. As one would expect, it was a very fast city, if you know what I mean. Everything was on the move and in a hurry and everyone was on the move. These included all the swindlers and all the crooks.

Getting to the city was one thing, but knowing how to locate her was another. It was obviously going to be easier to pick out a needle from a haystack than to find that lady in this sprawling city. He did not even know her name except for the fact that he belatedly wrote down her license plate number.

It was already mid afternoon when he sighted the city which was situated on top a plateau. It was for this reason that the climate here was always on the cool side. His first gamble was to seek out the most expensive hotel there and he found that out from the attendant in a gas station. She had looked very sophisticated and so it was not possible for her to be anywhere else, or at least so he thought. It was a very wild guess, but then if he were to be correct, it would be worth it.

He was able to locate the hotel. There he took a vantage position not far from its swimming pool from where he could see anyone that came in or left the facility. He idled around there for the rest of the day and well into the night while watching out for her. A lot of pretty women were there, especially around the swimming pool, and as a man who was used to the finer things of life as well as a couple of things about women, he knew that most of them were actually and not proverbially 'fishers of men'. Vanessa was however not one of them. Vanessa was the name that he had suddenly assigned to her.

To Johnny, Venus was the goddess of love and she was very pretty. To him this unknown lady was prettier than Venus, though he had never seen her, and it was for that reason that he chose the name Vanessa, which he thought, was derived from the name Venus. He could not tell whether that was the best name to choose but it sounded just right to him. Anyway one name was always as good as the other. He had thought of Aphrodisiaca before Vanessa, but that seemed to sound too erotic.

It was getting way into the night when he decided to go in for a late dinner. He was still watching out for her, though he knew deep within him that it was of no use. The first day of his quest was therefore over and he was disappointed. He hoped to take up room there later for the night. He had finished his dinner before he went over to the bar for a nightcap.

There was one pretty lady who had been eyeing him all day long and she came over to the bar to introduce herself to him. He knew what she was. She was one of those fishers of men. The day was gone and she had not come across even a half customer. The economy was bad and that had translated into bad business for them too. Everyone, especially the group that made up their clientele was now on the frugal part.

"Hello handsome? Is this seat taken?" That was how most of them started off. She was rather sophisticated, but what other class does one expect to meet in such a high-class hotel.

"No. It is not taken."

"And you?"

"Me?"

"Yes, you. I hope you are not taken too?"

He smiled because it was only then that he got the meaning of that question.

"Oh no, I am still as free as air."

"Me too." That was what he had suspected all along.

"Do you stay here?" He asked.

"Yes, on the fourth floor, and you?"

"No. I was just planning to check in."

"I had seen you all day long why hadn't you checked in since then? Were you waiting for someone?"

"Yes, but he did not turn up. I was waiting for my business associate." He was of course lying.

"I guess that there is no need to check in now."

"Why?"

"You are invited up to my room for the night. I don't quite like sleeping alone."

"What would that cost me?"

"If you insist, then you can always refund the money for the room and maybe add whatever else you wish to add."

"Baby, you just got yourself a deal."

"Mind you a couple of things would be on the house, but you just have to pay for the rest." He knew that it was a trap. She was a shrewd businesswoman and she intended to extort as much as possible from him.

"Like what and what?"

"Why don't you leave those for the later?"

"What drink would you like to have?"

"Just Vodka on the lime."

Johnny was already thinking of the following day and how he would locate Vanessa when the lady broke his chain of thoughts.

"You have not told me your name yet sweetie."

"Johnny."

"I am Joyce."

"I know."

"How come you know? Have we met before?"

"No, but I remembered when one of the barmen called you Joyce about an hour ago."

"Okay. That was actually the hotel manager. He was only helping out at the bar because one of his men called out from work."

"What exactly do you do for a living?"

"I am actually a business executive."

"What business are you into, if I am not being too inquisitive?"

"Hospitality."

"Not bad at all."

"And you?"

"I am a travelling salesman."

"And what do you sell?"

"Mainly ideas for other companies, but I also sell condoms as a side line."

"Condoms?"

"Sure condoms."

"But that does not require a salesman to market it."

"That sort of sounds right, but we are marketing a new type."

"I see. Do you have a few samples?"

"No. My business partner will bring them in whenever he turns up."

Not quite long after that discussion, she took a full-throated yawn to indicate that she was already too tired before saying:

"It seems that it is getting too late, why don't we go up to my place and at least try to get to know each other better?"

"You just read my thoughts."

They got off the stools at the bar counter and decided to walk up the stairs to the fourth floor. She claimed that she had a phobia for elevators, and they were at her door in no time at all. It seemed as if each of them was in a hurry to get there. She fished out the key to the room from her pocket book, unlocked the door and they went in. It was room four hundred and one, and it was exactly four floors up from the swimming pool. It looked as if the swimming pool was built just below it and by the side.

As soon as they stepped in, she wheeled around and planted one heck of a kiss on his lips. It was that wet passionate variety. It was also the tongue probing type and he enjoyed it. He did not fail to notice that she was pretty in her own right and she was very mild mannered to go with it.

She shed her clothing like a molting insect as she quickly made her way for the bathroom, and in no time at all he could hear the shower running. She invited him in so that they could have their bath together, but he declined. He had insisted that he felt too shy to try that and so she commented:

"Don't tell me that you have never seen a naked woman before."

"I have, but not one as pretty as you are." She giggled in delight before saying:

"In that case you had better come right in."

"No, thanks."

"Okay then, but please can you come over and help me scrub my back. It is itching me right at the center."

"Okay then."

Of course it was all lies. She just wanted him in there and he knew it. He was reluctant to go in there and only heavens could tell why. He did not have any cogent reason not to go in. In fact he did not have any reason at all. As soon as he went in and saw what he saw, he knew that he should have said yes right at the beginning.

It was her breasts that struck him first. They were the most outstanding feature of her entire body. They seemed natural though they could have been augmented, but what did that matter? They were each just shy of the size of a small personal watermelon, and that just made them perfect for her size. The teats were dark colored with what looked like Goosebumps around them and they tended to point upwards as if struggling to ascend to the skies. He did not waste any more time before he began to undress, but she stopped him:

"Why undress?"

"I don't want to get my clothes wet."

"I'll be careful. Just scrub my back."

He took the sponge that was offered to him and began to gently scrub her back. Before any of them knew what was going on, his palms were already planted squarely over her breasts. He gently touched and rubbed the nipples and they responded by further stiffening right away. Those Goosebumps seemed to even increase in number. She then drew his head closer and planted another kiss where it should be planted.

She then feverishly took one of his hands and moved it to somewhere between her legs. He immediately began to search. No one could be sure of what he was searching for, but he quickly withdrew his hand and began to pull down his pants in a hurry. My guess is that he had found whatever it was that he was looking for down there. Some embarrassing protrubation did not help matters. They made it harder for his pants to drop off to the floor. At that moment she reminded him of what she had said before:

"So far it has been on the house, but if you wish to go further then you might have to pay for that."

"Okay." That was all the answer that she could extract from him. He was already too far gone and excited to care. It took his hurriedly shaking hands to help get those damned pants to the floor.

"But you haven't asked how much it will cost you."

"Okay, how much?"

"A thousand."

"Okay."

"Before tax and tips."

"Okay."

She had got him where she wanted him. His voice betrayed the fact that he was in a hurry and his hands were also shaking in anticipation. Many of these ladies of the night knew how to play this game and she was an expert at it. He was too far gone to care anymore.

He was now in the showers with her and his fingers did not waste time before they resumed their search for whatever it was they were searching for or had found between her legs earlier on. His fingers suddenly, though slowly or maybe it was just the result of an accidental exploration, slid into her. It could have been by chance but it could have also been by design. At the same time his thumb played on her clit as if it was a guitar string. It was now very stiff and he was both slow and gentle while brushing over it. He was an expert at that.

A deep moan mingled with an even deeper sigh of relief and resignation from her was all he needed to know that he was on the right track. They found themselves on the floor of the bathroom without knowing how they got there. She was now gyrating and quaking uncontrollably as if she was having convulsions. It was at this point that he withdrew his fingers and hurriedly though deftly slid his manhood into her.

She moaned uncontrollably and sweated profusely. The loudest moans came when they climaxed together in unison, and it came from both of them. Her womanhood constricted as it tightened and loosened over his own as each let out a complete compliment of whatever juice they could. As she tried to hold him even tighter, especially with her legs to make sure that he did not slide out of her, he exploded once more. She exploded in response, and it was the second time in a few seconds that they had reached what could have gone for a well-choreographed common orgasm, but it was all for real.

They held tightly to each other for a few more minutes, each as exhausted as a flat tire, before they got off the floor to finish their showering and finally they dried up. No one spoke a single word, but the looks on their faces said it all. It was that satisfying look of one who had been to either heaven or paradise and had just come back from there. They went straight for the bed, and before one could intone 'Abracadabra', they were both fast asleep under the comforter. They slept like babies, looking innocent and all that—maybe deceptively so.

Johnny was the first to wake up and it was already way past eight in the morning. She was still fast asleep and it looked as if she was smiling in her sleep. He did not want to complicate issues and so he quietly dressed up and slid out of the room, just like the wind that he was after. This did not however take place until after he had left a wad containing two thousand dollars on the dressing table for her. He had made all those promises under duress as his lawyer would put it, but he had to make good of his promise.

A man who made promises under that type of duress was not obliged to make good of his promise. For Johnny however, who happened to be a perfect gentleman, a promise is a promise, no matter under what conditions they were made. Anyway, those promises were not exactly made under duress.

Johnny had already planned what his next move was going to be. He was very sure that it was going to help him catch up with his wind.

After her BMW had driven off he had, though belatedly, taken notice of its plate number and he had written it down. It was slightly misty then, but he was of the opinion that he saw it well, though he could have seen it better if he had tried to do so when she was still very close to him. He had written down the number and it was:

$$85122n6021$$

What he did was to head straight for the police station. There he reported that he had met a lady the previous night, but she had forgotten her pocket book in his room. He claimed that she gave him her name and address but that he accidentally lost them and so he wanted to find out how to get to her. According to him, he knew the tag number for her car and the make. He gave them the information, but they were not able to arrive at any identification.

The number was wrong because it was distorted and only partially visible through the thin mist that morning. The only thing that he was actually sure of was her face.

He had told them that the car was a BMW and he was right, but while they searched for a black one, it was actually a dark gray color. His mind was also so preoccupied with the thoughts of her face that he probably did not take in the finer details. His biggest blunder was that plate or tag number. He had mistaken the numbers for what they were not. Below again is what he had given to the police followed by the real number. That would show how he had mistaken them:

He had copied down: 85122N6021
Instead of: BS122NGOZI

It was a number that she had coined from her native name. Her name was NGOZI or blessing.

Johnny was out looking for Vanessa when her name was right there for him to copy. She had chosen that native name because she once had a girlfriend with the same name. Though she could not remember where she came from, she believed that she was a blessing to whoever hooked up with her.

In actual fact she was given birth to during a civil war in her country. Her mother was black while her father was a Caucasian mercenary. He was her father in that he was her biological father. The mercenary raped her mother and she became pregnant. When she had the baby it was a girl. She took heart and declared that God had blessed her with a healthy baby girl when others were having problems with carrying their pregnancies to full term. She therefore gave her the name Ngozi, or blessing. Interestingly enough she was considered barren before then. She had this child at the age of forty-five and Ngozi was her first and only child.

At the end of the war they found their way outside the country and they had lived there ever after till her mother passed away. Ngozi was therefore a half cast who took more after her father but also retained the best from each, as well as blending others to arrive at the best. She was terribly pretty. Her mother used to be a beauty queen and her father was once the winner of the Mister Universe contest and had also appeared as the 'most handsomest man alive' in one social magazine.

Combining these two was what gave birth to this awesome beauty. She was about six feet tall, which is on the tall side for a lady and she was so averagely built that her build was a perfect match for her height. Her skin was as smooth as silk with a color and tan that looked like a cross between egg white and olive, though more on the side of the white. Her hair came down in blond cascades to drape and adorn her swan-like neck. It barely touched her shoulders, but it came down in indeterminate coiffeurs which were each and collectively wavy. They bounced like the gentle waves of a natural cove or bay when she moved or flicked her head as she often did.

Her aquiline nose was a match for her face, just as if God had molded it specifically for her. Her azure blue eyes had a faint oriental slant to them. These were hardly perceptible, but they were there. They were equally penetrating and whenever she winked they tended to tell all sorts of stories. It might be better to stop describing her because that was how far he saw before she vanished from him. He only saw the rest from his minds eyes.

The only other thing is that her lips were well endowed and very kissably inviting. Though well endowed, those lips were just right for her and they added to her beauty. All said and done, it was a face that could make the heavenly dwellers turn around for a second look and at times wish that they were not living in heaven. She always tended to freak out her admirers. That was one disadvantage of being very pretty. Most men who would like to hit on her would see her as being way off and above their league.

In other words, most men will find it rather uncomfortable, if not afraid, to chat her up. That was the reason why she had not been married so far. The men never came to her, and the few that she dated were a few daring never do wells. It is a well known fact that while the pretty ones waited for their beauty to attract the men, it is the ugly ones, who being aware of their deficiencies, that put in extra effort and persevered by going to the men. The vice versa is also true with the men. This lends credence to the statistical rumor that most marriages happen to be between pretty and ugly couples.

Now that his plan with the police did not work out he was not sure of what to do next. He however remembered that admonition to try, try and try again. He therefore decided to go to the mall. Vanessa was the type that could only go to the high-end stores. It was for that reason that he made it to the central mall where most of the high-end stores were.

There were many shops there, but one of them stood out. It was a small but expensive store that sold expensive clothing and jewelry. Only the rich and the sophisticated were likely going to shop there. He was convinced that if he staked out that store he was very likely going to see her one of these days. It was not a store for the general of the mill type who were everywhere. As he saw the few that dared to walk into the store he knew that he was right. They were well dressed and each tended to carry himself or herself very high.

He took a vantage point not too far away in one of the many lounges and from there he watched the store all day long. He did not fail to notice that a lot of chicks, as well as men, who were there had not come to make purchases. They were there only to fish out each other.

By late evening he had become the target for a few of the ladies that were there. Just as had been pointed out much earlier on, the recession had taken its toll on most of their regular clientele. Many were now only out for essential goods while others never come there any longer. Most of them would wait till the shops are about to close down before making any desperate moves. By this time they will go with whoever came their way rather than go empty handed for the day.

It was still early spring and the weather was still struggling to warm up. It was becoming cold and the day was over. For Johnny, it was a disappointing day, and for many of the girls and women that he saw there, it was equally disappointing.

He was only in a light jacket and he knew that it was time to find a hotel where he would lodge for the night.

The air was already on the nippy side when he stepped outside, and it was at that time that he heard a voice call out from behind him:

"Excuse me sir, can you help me?"

"With what?" He replied as he wheeled around to see who owned that sweet voice that had called out to him.

He was not too sure of why it was so, but most of the women in this area were rather beautiful, and as for this one, he did not mind helping out at all.

"Please do you have a lighter or match that I could use to light a cigarette?"

"I am sorry to disappoint you. I am not a smoker."

"As for me, I have tried a couple of times to quit this nicotine thing, but I often got caught up once more in the craze."

"Have you ever tried nicotine gum or patches?"

"No."

"Why not try them?"

"When I asked for them, my doctor refused. He insisted that they had nothing to do with quitting. According to him, no matter what one tried, the final determinant is will power. He also insisted that moving from cigarettes to nicotine was just like going for the lesser of two evils. Why not go for no evil at all. He insisted that after all it was the nicotine in the cigarette that makes it addictive and so why go for the nicotine and insist on going off the addiction once and for all?"

"He has a point there." He thought for a while and then asked another question:

"What of those smoke free varieties?"

"They only managed to increase my craving."

"And finally what of those prescription tablets? I have heard of one that they called Chantix."

"I have tried it and it did not work for me."

"In other words the only alternative left for you is your will power?"

"That's all I have left."

"Maybe if you start to stay away from other smokers it might help to boost your will power."

"In that case can I stay with you?"

"I wouldn't have minded, but unfortunately I don't live here."

"I know that because I have never seen you here before. By the way where did you come from?"

"I came from the university town far away to the east."

"I knew it. I can always smell out an academician fro far away."

"But I have not said that I was into the academics."

"What do you do there then?"

"I am just a general contractor that services the school."

"In that case they have rubbed off on you. What have you come here for then?"

"I am on vacation and I just came visiting."

"A relation?"

"No. No one in particular. Just a plain adventurer."

"And where do you stay?"

"No where for now."

"What of my place then? At least for the night" He knew what she was up to and he was up to it too.

"I would accept, but I also know that nothing goes for nothing, so what will that cost me?"

"Nothing much. I just happen to like you."

"Just for the night?"

"Yes, just for the night, unless you want to stay longer then that could be arranged."

"And where do you live?"

"Not far from here."

"Let's go then."

Johnny had abandoned his bike and so they simply strolled through the cool night towards the suburbs where she lived. It was not far away as she had said, and she was right. It was a very small but well built house. It contained just two rooms, a kitchen and a bathroom. One of the rooms acted as her sitting room. Just as she was rummaging through her handbag for her keys he suddenly asked:

"Would you like me to carry you across the threshold?"

A smile of understanding immediately lit up her face as she curdled and snuggled against him to keep warm. She nodded as an affirmation. As soon as the door was opened, he lifted her up in his arms with ease and strode into the room. She stretched out her arm and switched on a red light while he kicked shut the door with the heel of his foot. He then looked down into her eyes and she immediately did what he had expected her to do. She quickly locked her lips on to his own.

He let her down softly on the sofa. From all he had gathered from her, she was a final year medical student in a nearby institution. Was this a normal job for medical students? Or was it just the most popular reason that they gave to be there. If it were a nurse, he would probably understand. It was claimed, though wrongly, though at times rightly too, that those nurses were to medical doctors what the reverend sisters were to the reverend fathers. I cannot swear that I know exactly what they are to each other. When once I asked a Reverend mother what that relationship was, she only asked me to read her lips. She shut them very tight. She then got up and offered him a bottle of beer from the fridge. As he sipped his beer she left for a shower.

When she came out of the bathroom, she was glowing with smiles, but he could not imagine why it was so. It was now his turn, and she was going to warm up some dinner while he did so.

By the time he came out, the dining table was already set. It was for two and it was complete with candles. A candle light dinner was not part of what he had expected and she was already seated on the table waiting for him. He was already famished and so he sat down right away. As for the before meal grace, all she did was to make a sign of the cross and say:

"Minus Satan plus God."

"Amen." They both intoned in unison and started eating right away.

The dish was made up of vegetable salad tossed together with fried chicken and boiled quail eggs. There were diced carrots, beets and shitake mushrooms; while the vegetable contained cully flowers, cabbages and Romaine lettuce. The salad cream was left on one side and there was a small vial of extra virgin olive oil. For desert, it was vanilla flavored non-fat Greek Yogurt. As for table wine, she had opted for fine champagne. She surely knew how to dine well.

He ate a few mouthfuls and stopped. He watched on as she ate. When she noticed that, she asked him:

"Why are you not eating? Don't you like my cooking?"

"It's not that."

"What is the problem then?"

"For me, watching you eat is like eating itself."

"Please why don't you go ahead and eat rather tease me."

He then resumed eating. The food was indeed as delicious as she looked and he was right. Now it was his turn to break the silence:

"You told me that you are a medical student?"

"Yes and why do you ask?"

"Did you cook this food?"

"Yes I did."

"Are you a chef too?"

"That's what I did to raise money for medical school."

"I really respect you and I already envy whoever would be so lucky as to have the honor of being your husband."

"Thanks for all that."

He then continued with his food till the plate was empty. They then cleared the table and took the plates to the sink to wash them together. She washed the plates and he dried them. Somewhere along the line their hands unintentionally touched as she was handing a plate to him. It was but a very brief touch. That was however more than enough to do the trick. Not only did electricity develop between them, the current was so high that even sparks began to fly between the two.

As he looked into her eyes, he knew that lust had taken over. It was mutual. They wanted each other and they wanted each other badly. She did not resist, neither did she try to back away as those two palms went for those her two golden orbs. They were each struggling to shoot out of her "V-necked" negligee. She was delicate, soft, 'curlable' and shapely.

He could not tell how it all happened, but as he went for those two orbs, they suddenly jumped right out of that negligee of their own accord. He was not too sure of what to do with them though he quickly grabbed them. They were shaped like bananas though full with the nipples pointing upwards towards his mouth. He had no choice but to abandon the grab and go for them with his mouth. They were already stiff and they responded to the touch of his lips. He teased them with his tongue and then with his teeth and he could tell from her reaction how she felt. She held ever so tightly and almost squeezed the life out of him. As he brought up his head from her bosom for a breather, she pleadingly planted one heck of a kiss on his lips and that further put him on fire.

Just like when he carried her across the threshold, he did so one more time, but this time around he was in a hurry. He was in too much of a hurry to make it to the sofa not to talk of the bedroom. He hurriedly, though gingerly put her on the counter top next to the sink; having brushed away whatever was there to the floor. She hung tightly to his neck still trying to plant one type of kiss or the other, and they came in quick succession.

He still hung on to her lips when his fingers located those damn nipples once more. She shivered and surrendered herself completely. She now lay back on the counter top with her fingers attempting to grasp the water pipes. He then hurriedly tore off her negligee as well as his own nightdress. His fingers then went further down, and as soon as he touched whatever it was that he touched, she began to moan and cry out loudly. She spoke in tongues so he was not able to recount what it was that she said. He could no longer wait, for he was almost at his own climax, She was at hers too. He penetrated and right away, they both began to jerk and moan incoherently. They both broke into sweat as all their muscles tightened and loosened in very quick succession as one would expect during a convulsion.

They had reached their peak at the same time and the counter top quaked in rhythm to the activity that was going on over it. Both man, woman and counter had all quaked as they reached and realized their individual and collective goals in an apparent crescendo!

It was a sort of an unintentional earthquake of a very low magnitude that was not detectable on the Richter scale. The epicenter of this quake was somewhere around the edge of the counter top and somewhere lower down their bodies. They each breathed very heavily as their sweat mingled.

It was only after this that they were able to behold each other's eyes. They were tired and utterly exhausted and each begged for rest. They both collapsed onto the floor and slept off till the wee hours of the morning. Just before she slept off, she had weakly, but happily informed him that it was the very first time in her life that she had experienced up to five different orgasms all at once.

By the time they got up, it was early Sunday morning. This girl was the type that, even if she did not go for Fridays confession, would go to church on Sunday to pray for the forgiveness of her sins through the week. She considered most of those sins as sins of necessity. Johnny had not asked her what was her name for only one reason. Most of the ladies who went out like that always ended up with fake names.

She had told him of her own volition that her name was Angela, but the bible on the dressing table with her photograph in it told a different story. She was Francesca, as it was pronounced.

To Johnny he had just met an Italian, though anyone could have that name. He even tried to imagine that he had just gotten himself involved with men of the underworld.

No wonder she was an avid church attendee. Even the mafia dons never took going to the church on Sundays lightly and that explained why she was stuck on leaving for the church so early.

They quickly dressed up and left the house. She was headed for the Roman Catholic Church while he headed for the Pentecostal mega church that was not too far off. He was not the church going type, but this lady had got him to try it. His plan was to return to her place after service and then continue with his quest for the wind from there.

At the church door there was a notice to the effect that the preachers wife died that morning. They had therefore decided to honor her by cancelling the service for that day. It was however going to be held the following day. They were going to honor one of their illustrious members during that service too. They expected many dignitaries to attend and he actually imagined that it could be a ripe forum for Vanessa.

When he left the church, he had nowhere to go and so he made his way once more to another high-class hotel. Soon after he came in, he saw this very young and innocent looking girl. She was there most of the day and it puzzled him as to what such a young girl could be doing there. She looked sixteen or even less, though looks could once in a while be deceptive. She was most probably also a novice when it came to the affairs of the heart.

Johnny was however about to receive a shock that evening. He had not expected it, but she had come over to him of her own volition. Was she a product of child prostitution? Was she being forced into the slave sex market? When she spoke, her voice was as revealing as her face. She looked confused and her voice was haltingly shaky, but she seemed determined at whatever it was that she wanted.

"Good evening sir." She had greeted in that innocent child-like voice.

"Good evening. What could your name be?"

"Jacinta."

"How old are you?"

"Twenty four." He did not believe her at all.

"And what are you doing here?"

"Why all the interrogation?"

"It's not an interrogation as such. I just wanted to make sure that I am not messing with a minor."

A smile then came to her face as she began to muster a little more confidence. It was however a shy type of smile.

"People always make that mistake of thinking that I am far younger than I really am."

"In that case I am no exception."

"Back to the answer to your question, I am just waiting for my mother."

"Where is she? You have been here for more than a while."

"In this hotel somewhere. She had asked me to pick her up. I drove the car to school for extra lessons but the classes were cancelled today and so I had to come in early."

"So you are a student?"

"Yes, I am."

"And what is your field of study?"

"Pre-marital concupiscence," He was satisfied. He had expected her to say that she was a medical student.

"Is that a course of study?"

"Of course. It deals with all sorts of pre—as well as post-marital indiscretions amongst both men and women."

"I hope you are not here for the practicals?"

"Not yet, but that was part of why I came over to you."

"How can I help you then?"

"Can you start by buying me a drink?"

"Sure, and which would you like?"

"Straight cognac if you don't mind."

"You must have quite a sophisticated taste."

"That is my mothers favorite, and it was from her that I caught up with it."

"It is not a bad choice anyway."

He ordered two glasses of straight fine champagne cognacs. Most of the seats were now empty and so they sat on one of them by the corner.

"You have not told me what your mother does here."

"She works here as the chief chef."

"Nice job."

"So they claim."

There was a small lull in the conversation before Johnny spoke again:

"Tell me something."

"What?"

"You still haven't told me the exact reason why you came over to me."

Her demeanor immediately changed. It looked as if she was beginning to feel guilty of something. He knew why. It was surely her first time of trying to pick up a man from the hotel. He therefore decided to help her out:

"It seems as if you have not done this before."

"No, I have not." He was sure of that and he knew how she was felling. For any normal person, she would wish that the earth could open up right now and swallow her.

"Is it also going to be your first time, if you understand what I mean?"

"Yes."

"So the story about your mom is also not true."

"Yes."

"So why do you want to go into this type of life?"

"Actually I am in medical school and about to go into my last semester, but there is no money left to continue."

"My question still stands. Why this very type of life?"

"It is the quickest way to make a lot of money to pay off those staggering school fees."

"I see."

"No you don't see. One can only understand my predicament if he had been through it himself."

"Trust me, I understand."

"I have been here all day long and I was afraid to go out with anyone. A couple of men had tried to chat me up but I was reluctant to try it out. When I saw you, it was however a different story. You stirred up something within me and I could not tell what it was,"

"Desire?"

"Yes, but it must be something more than that."

"Can I help you out?"

"Yes."

"Love?"

"Very likely."

"You are not sure?"

"How could I be sure? I am not exactly the social type and I have never had any feelings for any man before."

"Don't tell me that you are also still a virgin."

"Well, I am."

"Trust me, this is not the right place to loose it."

"I know that, but it is just that desperate situations always call for desperate measures. I can at least always remember that I did so to become a medical doctor."

"I had noticed both the reluctance as well as the desperation, on your face."

"It took monumental effort as well as super human resolve for me to come over to you."

"So what exactly do you want to do?"

"I am ready to go with you for the night if you will give me enough money."

"How much do you consider as enough?"

She seemed to think over it for some time before coming up with a stunning answer:

"Please forget the money aspect of it all."

"Why?"

"My feelings towards you will not let me accept even a cent from you for that."

"In that case you will not be able to graduate."

"I am aware of that. When I saw you my heart went into instant flutter and my mind told me that this was it."

"Was what?" He had asked this question as if he did not know what she was talking about.

"Love."

"Looks as if it is mutual."

Deep within him, Johnny had a lot of pity for this young innocent girl. Not only was he actually a bachelor at heart, but he was also still after Vanessa. His heart was already spoken for and it was by Vanessa. This was however not one of those opportunities that a man would like to miss.

He was split between deceiving this innocent intelligent girl and simply helping her out. She, on her part was split between love and money. Necessity seemed to have initially gotten a better hold of her judgments. He would probably have just helped her out, but what wrong would be done if he simply enjoyed himself for the evening and then continued the following morning on his quest?

The nagging problem was what he would do to her mind. To him, it was going to be a one-night stand, but to her it was going to be the beginning of a long-term relationship. He finally decided to go for it. After all life is full of different experiences both good and bad; just as there were successes and failures. Life is replete with all sorts of ups and downs and so it did not really matter at the end. He was only going to help show her one of those experiences—that of disappointment. He was still deep in those thoughts when she drew closer and asked:

"Are you married?"

"No, but why do you ask?"

"Nothing. It's good to know that." She now looked more relaxed and surer of herself.

"Do you have a girlfriend?"

"Yes, but not a steady or serious one."

"What of me?"

"You might be the one."

With that answer she got even closer to him. And she was shaking slightly as if she was afraid. Once more he decided to help her out. He put his hand around her shoulder, drew her closer to him and gave her a peck on the cheek. It was just a peck but it served its purpose. Blood immediately flew to her face as she blushed. It was that coy type of blushing and she looked away from him. It was obvious that she was still a novice when it came to such matters.

He did not ask her before ordering another set of drinks. As soon as the drinks arrived and they began to drink he started off with another conversation. This time around, it was with a purpose.

"I am usually an early bird, but it's because of you that I am still awake."

"Quite unlike me, I usually read a lot at night and go in very late."

"That's understandable."

"Can we go up to your place after this set of drinks?"

She asked this question while looking away. It was obvious that she was very nervous about what was going to take place, though eager for it. It was only then that he excused himself and went to book for a room.

"Okay." He answered when he returned, and that made her even more nervous. It was obvious that she was about to go into an incidence that she might not be able to forget for the rest of her life and she should be nervous. Her fingers were beginning to fidget.

Johnny drained whatever was left in his glass and got up. She followed suite though more slowly as well as reluctantly. She was eager though. To make her feel more at ease, he had decided on taking a walk with her. They walked out of the building and off into the night for a short stroll.

They walked hand in hand, hardly ever talking to each other. The idea was to get her to feel more at ease. The weather was on the verge of getting nippy and the wind very calm. The moon was about full and it silvery rays made her face look even prettier when he glanced sideways at her. The night was also becoming damp though there was no rain.

An owl hooted from a branch not too far away from them. The hoot did not sound quite normal and Johnny began to laugh.

"What makes you laugh like that?" She asked.

"Because of what that owl was saying."

"What did it say, if you have the ability to interpret hoots?"

"I thought that I heard it say something like—what do these two love birds think they are doing out here so late?"

That was enough to make her laugh too. She was already beginning to feel more at ease with him as his hand moved from her back where it had been for some time now to her waist.

The sky was very clear and cloudless and a lot of stars were there to be seen as they spangled the entire celestial dome. He watched them and then pointed out one of them to her:

"Do you see that very bright star towards the southern horizon?"

"Are you talking about that one that seems to be moving faster than the rest?"

"Yes. It is one of our satellites."

"How do you know that?"

"That's my field of study."

"By the way, you have not told me what you do for a living. All that I am sure of is that you are a gentleman and that you must be in a very responsible position."

"I studied astronomy as well as astrology, but my post graduate field was business administration. For now I am the chief executive officer of a computer chips industry."

"I would have though that one had to be involved in that field to head such an industry?"

"By the time one gets to the top he does not have to know anything about the field he is in."

"That does not seem to make a lot of sense to me."

"When it comes to the post of Chief Executive Officer, one could even be a complete dunce and yet be the best. His job is to find and make money for the industry. It is his influence that matters. If for instance they wanted money for a project he might be able, because of his influence, get a bank to loan them the money very easily. As for sales, he might have others who would like to pay him back by patronizing his company. That is why you might find most of them idling about in golf clubs."

"Now I see what you mean, but it seems to be unfair to the real professionals."

"It might seem quite unfair, but do not forget that the name of the game is money."

"You have a point there."

It was beginning to get very nippy and so he let her drape his jacket over her shoulder, while she snuggled against him to let him have some of the heat that was being generated by his jacket. They then made their way back to the hotel. A gust of wind blew and a whistling pine tree that they just passed made its whistling noise. She was the person who laughed this time around.

"Why are you laughing?" he asked her.

"I was just wondering what you would say that you heard the pine tree say this time around."

"I happen to know exactly what it had in mind."

"I am not very sure that trees have a mind, but what could that be?"

"Trust me. It saw you. You looked rather beautiful, especially under the influence of the mellow moon. And it cat-called."

That was enough to extract a loud uncontrollable laughter from her.

"Are you always so funny?" She asked while still laughing.

"Actually I wasn't trying to be funny. I was merely stating the fact."

"What fact?"

'The fact that you are very beautiful."

"But it is how you put it that makes me laugh."

"Believe it or not. It is your presence that extracts that quality from me. I am not usually that way."

"Thanks and I believe you."

He then wheeled her round and embraced her while looking her straight into the eyes at close quarters. He saw what he had expected. Her eyes were on fire with desire and he knew that he had achieved that goal of keeping her calm and assured. A very passionate kiss followed. He could not quite remember who initiated it.

Her eyes were closed tight as she lifted up her face to get to his lips. He was famed for being one hell of a kisser. She let him explore her entire oral cavity with his tongue and she tried the same, all the while leaving her eyes shut in order to savor the experience.

By the time he withdrew his lips, she was still facing upwards with her eyes still closed. It was just as if she was expecting some more. Maybe, it was just that she had forgotten where she was, or most likely, she did not want to open those eyes and loose that fascinating experience. In reality, it was her first full passionate kiss. The only thing that managed to escape her lips was a very subdued: "Thank you."

They were around the entrance of the hotel and so they just quietly moved on to his room, which happened to be on the ground floor there. He unlocked the door and they went in. He asked her to go in for a shower and she did so while he went in for his own after her. Then came a nightcap. It was more cognac. This last one was just enough to loosen her inhibitions and she was ready for him as he put off the lights. It was at this moment that he heard her say something that made him realize that she was still not fully at ease:

"Please try and be gentle with me."

"I know that, and I will."

Having assured her of that in order to increase her confidence, he went to work on her. A little kiss was all he needed before his hands went down to her breasts. They were rather small, just the size of very large lemons, but they were very firm. He was not sure of which was more firm, the breasts or the nipples. He romanced them and then sucked away. As he did so he could feel her tensing and tightening up. That meant that she was beginning to enjoy it. He then let his hand fall down to her groin area and she recoiled slightly without pulling away.

He gently searched without going in and he found what he was looking for. As soon as he began to work on her clit, she began to moan and writhe all about. He did not want to overdo it, but she was already beginning to get very wet. Then she got so excited that she suddenly began to urinate. He did not mind that because he was beginning to loose control too.

He was now on top of her and she held tightly to him. He then introduced himself into her. It was a very slow and deliberate introduction and he had not even gone far enough when he ejaculated. She did not feel any pains as such, but even if she did, it was going to be a sweet and welcome type of pain. Her fluid was everywhere and as soon as his own was pumped into her she reacted. She moaned aloud and came once more. She struggled to hold tight onto him while he collapsed in a heap besides her.

He did not want to see what she would look like when she woke up in the morning. In other words he did not want to see her face when she got disappointed in the morning. He did not wait for the day to fully break before he left. He left her alone still asleep like a baby on the bed, but it was only after he had left some money for her. She had claimed that she needed about eighth thousand dollars to complete her school fees. He left a check for twelve thousand dollars for her and vanished into the thin air, just like that wind that he was chasing after. He was sure that the amount would help to ease her mind.

He strolled around in the town till about seven in the morning before he headed for the church. Somehow or the other, the fact that dignitaries were going to be there was enough to make him go there.

It was at this time that he once more thought of Vanessa in terms of love and he remembered a poem that he had once read that tended to reflect on what he felt about her:

An Ode to Love

A hundred days is like but a while to you O Love
Though a day like a thousand often could.
This is love that comes from deep within,
Love that no mockery knows—
A feeling that's so pleasant and so wonderful yet
So powerful that hatred fizzles into it—love.
Love knows no hatred but is
Full of simplicity and immense wisdom, yet blind.

Oh how I love you, my precious love
Love that no vanity ever knows.
It neither thinks evils nor wrongs at all
And's so pleasant it obsesses the mind
As very often it does ravish it.
Oh thou forgiving love!
Who often is strife to strife itself
How I wish and yearn for you.

Oh fairest of all the loves!
You are past all comparison
As a shield over my enfeebled mind.
How you bestir me from within oh love!
Awaken not nor bestir my feelings no more
As you come skipping into me as love
To spirit away my erstwhile woes.
Do remold my tender feelings with your tender care
O fair and devoted spirit.
Come back in your spotless guise
To ravish my heart espoused to your love
Fully perfumed beyond earthly fancies.

O thou fountain of love,
Thou fountain of want:
How fair, how pleasant.
O my love of all delights
How without you darkness enshrouds my soul.
Thou humble solace that is my love
Your steadfastness all odds do overcome.
Your inordinacy knows no bounds,
You great and mighty emotion,
O you fulfiller of all my wants.
Enslave me into your endearing love
That I might stay with you to eternity.

There's always a time to love,
Though a time for hate occasionally comes;
Love that's full of joy and hope.
So full of patience and peace,
So perfect, so pure,
So full of meek and tender love
That your goodness comfort does bring
So full of compassion, so full of grace;
Your consuming fire so pure
It ennobles and mellows my heart.
Your thoughts as sweet as honey is my love
It turns all vanity into hope.
O honorable love
Deepest of all emotions
Proof of all sincerity
How for your tender presence I yearn O love!

That was how he saw Vanessa in his minds eye. She had become the object of his existence and the apple of his eyes. She was now love itself, or maybe the goddess of love on earth.

Wonders will never end!

He strode into the church, as the service was about to end. As a newcomer to that church, or rather as a guest worshipper if that was what he went there for, he preferred to sit at the back. From there he could see and observe what was going on all around. It was a very big and cozy edifice with two layers of seats for the congregation. It was so big that it could very easily seat up to three thousand members. That was one of the reasons that it was considered a mega church. Surprisingly the place was as good as full.

He knelt down for a very shot prayer before sitting down to listen to the announcements. It was at that moment that he beheld what he did not want to believe at first. There sat the wind that he had been after!

Vanessa was seated to the left of the Bishop in the altar. The bishop had come from his bishopric some five hundred miles away to minister onto his flock. From all that he saw, she was the Bishops wife. The preacher in that particular church, the one whose wife had died a day earlier, was seated on the other side of the Bishop. He was actually an Arch—Bishop, though there were no other Bishops between him and the other pastors.

His mind was in turmoil with a mixed bag of feelings. He had eventually caught up with his wind, but she was the wife to the Arch—Bishop. He was happy at having found her, but he was rather sad that she was already taken.

This was the house of God and so not the right place for him to harbor such thoughts, but then who knows? She might still be available though that possibility was as good as improbable.

That was all that occupied his mind till the service ended about fifteen minutes after he came in. He remembered when the Bishop made a short speech but he did not hear even a single word of what he said. He was a very powerful and motivating speaker and many considered him the best orator of modern times, but had no effect on him. His eloquence had been wasted on him. He was there in person, but both his mind and his ears were somewhere else and far away.

The collection of offerings was the final activity before everyone headed for the doors. They all had to dance to the front of the altar to do so in the presence of the preacher. Johnny believed that this arrangement was there just to make the donors too ashamed to drop small amounts into the offering plates; after all this was church business as most of them will put it. Just as Johnny was dropping in his offering, their eyes met! He was very eager to search out her thoughts.

Her face had remained expressionless, but there was a hidden smile of satisfied curiosity behind that façade. He knew that she recognized him and he knew that she wanted to tell him something. She was obviously happy to see him. He was of course not the type a lady would be in a hurry to forget. His father was the handsome man who created the first beauty pageant for women after he had won the handsome man's trophy for three consecutive years. His mother was the first winner of the pageant that he had organized. This would give one a faint idea of what he was like. They were both a match for each other for sure.

He was born and raised in luxury and tender care, but he grew up to become an independent and single-minded adventurer, as well as a bachelor at heart. He had had more than his own share of women and he had sown quite a few wild oats. Had they all germinated he would have long become the record setting owner and father of a clan, if not a tribe. It was the proliferation of various contraceptive devices that helped keep him in check. What I mean is that it was because of there that he never became the father of a tribe, or even maybe father of a nation, if not nations.

Just like Vanessa, he had blue eyes too, but his were of a very deep blue shade. They were uniquely and captivatingly shaped, and together with those nearly bushy eyebrows and masculine jaws and no single facial hair, he remained that type of hunk that was simply described as being 'all that'. He was muscular, but the muscles were in the right places, each pack well defined and yet they blended and merged with each other imperceptibly. In other words he had the physique and build of the Olympian gods.

His hair had been always cropped short and his upper torso tapered down in a 'V' figure from his broad shoulders down to his waist. His legs were athletically built and of a size that matched and complimented his six feet two inches height.

There is no need to talk about his face. It might suffice it to remember that he was called baby-face in school, and it had remained that way ever after. Like Peter Pan, he had refused to grow old.

For this reason, it was not surprising that when their eyes met, though she was seated in the holly of hollies, her heart skipped a couple of beats. She immediately recognized him as the man that she saw on the road a few days earlier. She had wanted to stop and pick him up, but she was afraid that from his looks she might fall in love with a total stranger and it was due to this confusion that she drove off. She had sort of fallen for him from that very brief encounter.

Her face lighted up and the ghost of a smile came to the edge of her luscious lips. Johnny knew that she had fallen for him, but his problem was that the Bishops wife was not one to mess around with. At first he was convinced that God will never forgive him for that, but then he remembered the case of King David and Uriah's wife. That was worse than what he had in mind and yet David was forgiven at the end. That was proof that God was an all forgiving and kind God and he was going to exploit that.

After he had dropped his money into the tray, he quietly went back to his seat at the back of the church. He was sure that she was watching. At the end of the service the officials went to the three doors to shake hands with and thank the congregants as they left. The Bishop was at one door, the preacher at another and Vanessa at the third. Of course he headed for Vanessa's exit. It was a golden opportunity for him.

When it got to his turn, he stretched out his hand and shook hers. It was as soft as velvet. Her voice was intriguingly mesmerizing as she intoned the usual 'God Bless You'. Her voice was like a perfect blend of alto and tenor with a faintly reverberating timbre to it. In other words, her voice was essentially like a choir or orchestra of its own and the pitch could never be more perfect.

He answered back; 'and you too'. As she heard his voice for the first time she swallowed hard before responding again. It was his voice that took her in. It was a slow deep baritone that tended to hang and linger awhile in the air of its own accord. He could see the longing in her eyes, but she had to be careful. He then continued without waiting for her to answer back:

"Good morning and a happy Monday your eminence."

"Eminence?"

"I am not too sure of how to address you but my guess is that it must be the right way to address a Bishop or his wife."

"Joy is the name"

"Good morning Joy."

"Or Ngozi, if you wish."

"Ngozi?"

"Yes. Ngozi. That means Blessing."

"What a nice name."

"Good morning and what might be your name?"

"Johnny Cash."

"You are not from this area?"

"No."

"Your first time in our church?"

"Yes."

"Haven't we met before?"

"Yes."

"Where?"

"My guess is that you remember, but lets save that till later."

"Room one thousand and six at the Hilton by two in the afternoon."

"Thanks."

With that brief encounter he moved on. He was now happy and satisfied as well as expecting, but he was also getting confused all at once. Why should the Bishops wife invite him to a room in the most exclusive Hotel around? That was however something that he was going to find out about much later.

By half past one in the afternoon he was already at the Hilton Hotel. The spring temperature was just right and there was no need for a jacket. It was slightly cloudy and cool and the birds were everywhere each piping out its own song with happiness. Their songs were enough to put off all miseries from any afflicted souls and gladden any hearts that heard them. At times their songs seemed so melancholic that he felt he was already on his way to meet his love.

The tree branches barely swayed to the gentle zephyrs as they cast only the ghosts of shadows from the hidden sun. The vista was lovely to behold, smooth and mellow, with nature at its best. The leaves were only beginning to come alive and they came in various shades of green, while the grass was beginning to respond the natures nourishing season. One lizard by the entrance turned and nodded his head at him. He knew that it was encouraging him to match in and claim his love.

This was the advantage of situating such a hotel at the suburbs. Many flowers were beginning to bloom and the calm winds were so gentle that even their gusts were only able to cause them to stir. Honeybees were everywhere as they buzzed in frenzy from one flower to the other. Many butterflies were also beginning to appear and they too were there feeding on and pollinating the flowers too.

Johnny sat down on a longue chair by the swimming pool that tended to arc around most of the hotel. He wanted to take in more of the beauty of the place. He was barely seated when that sleek BMW rolled in. He waited for a few minutes and then made it to the lobby to take the elevator to the tenth floor.

On the tenth floor he went straight for room 1006. On the handle was a sign that read: 'Do not disturb'. That was where he was asked to come and so he intended to disobey the sign. He waited for a few minutes and then timidly tapped on the door.

"Come right inside. The door is unlocked." It was her voice and he breathed a deep sigh of relaxation. He turned the knob cautiously and opened the door wide before stepping in.

"Good afternoon Joy." He greeted as he stepped in and carefully closed the door behind him.

"Good afternoon." She replied as she took a glance at her wristwatch. "It seems we are a little bit early."

"I couldn't wait."

"Me too, and how did you manage to trace me to this city and place?"

"I've tried all sorts of places and it was just a stoke of luck that brought me to the church. I have been frantically searching for you."

"By the way do you know why I did not stop for you that morning?"

"No, but why? I was devastated by that move."

"I wanted to pick you up but there was that inner feeling that asked me to make sure that I was not just about to pick up a killer."

"A nice decision."

"And why did you decide to look for me?"

"Haven't you ever heard the phrase 'love at first sight?'"

"Yes I have heard of it, and that was the first time that I had ever experienced it."

"You too?"

"Yes and it was abnormal."

"What will your husband say when he finds out that you are in love with another man?"

"Which husband?"

"The Bishop of course." That made her laugh aloud.

"For your information, I am single."

"You are getting me confused.

"I am not his wife. He is just a friend and a regular. He comes from the head quarters of the church far away and whenever he comes here, I double as his wife. I come from a city that is about halfway between this one and his own."

"So what do you do for a living normally?"

"I am into the escort business."

"Won't he start looking for you very soon?"

"No. They have all sorts of meetings and he will not be home till about three or four o'clock tomorrow morning. Whenever meetings have financial undertones they last very long. I will see him in the Bishops court tomorrow morning. This used to be his church before he moved to a much bigger one far away in New Haven. Here I am me, but over there in the church, I am his wife and live in the official residence with him."

"So why are you wasting time. Why don't we get on with it?

"But it's you who is wasting time by asking too many questions."

With that, they ran into each other's arms smooching as they met. Each was exploring the others oral cavities with his or her tongue as the case may be. From her mouth he changed to nipping her ear lobes with his teeth before beginning to kiss her neck. She was quite flexible, but he was in too much of a hurry to have a plan of what to do next. She felt the same way too. That feeling was mutual.

By the time they hit the sofa, they were each miraculously undressed. He could not believe his eyes! Her breasts were not very easy to describe. They were just the size of very large vidola oranges but at the same time they sort of looked faintly like bananas. Her nipples were extra dark and they were teasing him so he grabbed at them. The sizes of the breasts were just perfect for him. They filled his palms with a little surplus. As he gently squeezed away, she arched her back to offer him more of it while shivering from excitement from that shock of having been discovered so soon. He then teased the nipples and they almost instantly got as hard as stone.

He then went on to explore other essential zones. With that, she suddenly opened up her thighs. He did not waste time before he followed the cue. His fingers went straight for her center of gravity. How he managed what followed one could never explain, but two fingers had found their way inside her, one on her clitoris and yet another way up above that zone. One rubbed, one searched and the other pressed down. He had just discovered and switched on her G-zone. The effect was obvious. She moaned, and uttered all sorts of incoherent half sentences and phrases while writing all over the sofa. She was the Bishops wife and so he could understand why she spoke in tongues. He suspected that she was only giving testimonies in tongues.

He could no longer bear it and so he feverently penetrated. She shuddered in pleasure and let out an agonizingly sweet cry of joy. She came right away, maybe for the third time or so, and he did so too. The entire episode was a very short one, but it was full of passion as they collapsed into each other's arms.

Though they had collapsed into each other's arms, it was a very slight movement that got her on fire once more. When he looked into her eyes, what he saw in them was exactly what he felt himself. It was weakness and total helplessness both inextricably intertwined with desire. The Tiger in her had just been let loose by that act alone.

Though tired and apparently exhausted, she was able to roll him to his back before climbing on top. She sat astride over his lower portion and immediately, though with shaky hands reinserted his now erect manhood into her now burning oven. Now that she was on top and in charge she rode him as fiercely as a cowboy will ride a wild stallion. It was fast and ferocious and at top speed. He tried in vain to get a grab of her breasts as they jerked and bounced all about every which way to all her various antics. He therefore settled for her clitoris.

As he caressed it, she rode him even more fiercely and more wildly. She moaned, she grunted, she shouted and she testified all at once. He could not understand what she testified about since it was done haltingly in a hitherto unknown tongue. Warm sweat cascaded down all over him from all over her body just as that her internal came all over his mid area.

As soon as he felt himself further hardening, he unintentionally and spontaneously increased the intensity of that caress. He was tender to touch that area, but she was as wild as it could get. In no time at all it seemed as if she was gyrating in every given direction, and as soon as it seemed that she had got to supersonic rate he could hear the sonic boom as she broke the sound barrier and literarily found herself far into outer space or limbo. It was a land of bliss where tender feelings paradoxically merge with forceful activities. This led to a fairly protracted orgasmic episode that defies all description.

She arched her body wildly with muscles strung like a bow and then she exploded all over him. He exploded essentially at the same time too. For each of them, and for her in particular, what followed this was like a series of aftershocks from an earthquake. She came, and she came again uncontrollably.

She had lost count, but she had later confessed that it must have been an unbelievable series of over fifteen orgasms that had come both individually and collectively in series. It was a once in a life time experience that left her with only about a tenth of her energy to manage with. She had also explained that it was a blissful experience that defied any description.

Johnny had also experienced it. To him, he had chased his wind and he had found her, to her she had waited for a wind to come but this was one heck of a wind, it was an irresistible hurricane. She had been totally consumed by his passion.

It took a while before any of them could find their voice. They were each too weak to speak, laugh or even smile.

Eventually Joy was the first to speak:
"I am crazy about you Johnny."
"Me too. I might even be crazier."
It was only then that she sort of began to look a little bit shy though more graceful. A couple of nervous smiles began to creep across her face and right away he began to suspect that it was going to be a complicated relationship. He was a bachelor at heart and never wanted to get married. He did not however mind getting hitched to this one. It was the first time that he ever had that type of feeling.

"I hope that you realize that we have not yet formally introduced ourselves to each other?"

"I am aware of that, but does that really matter now that we have come to know and understand each other better?"

"You have a point there."

"Anyway I am not married, and I am the Chief Executive Officer of a computer chip industry in Neon City. I am on a thirty-day vacation and I decided to hike around town like an average Joe."

"So that's why you were flagging me down that morning?"

"Yes."

"Would you believe it if I told you that in our profession one, as a rule, should never get emotionally involved with her client. In your own case however it has come to be an exception."

"Is that another way of saying that you have fallen stupidly in love?"

"I have." This was said in a very slow and soft voice to reflect the earnestness in it. She was speaking from her heart. He immediately knew that she meant it and he was also afraid that he knew where she was heading. Incidentally, he felt the same way too.

"Let me confess something to you Joy."

"Go right away, I am your confessor."

"I am naturally a bachelor at heart and initially I was afraid to get too close to you."

"Why?"

"I was afraid that I might fall madly in love with you and maybe even loose my bachelorhood."

"Have you?"

"It seems so. I am sure that I have fallen in love with you. As I had pointed out before, it was love at first sight and it is total love."

"Lets get hitched then."

"I'll need some time to think about that part of it."

"How long would you need?"

"Just hold on a moment."

His heart and senses were in turmoil. He was not too sure that he wanted to get married, but then he would not let her go for any reason whatsoever. It was very hard to resist her.

It was now that he was able to see the entire package called Joy, and that did not help matters. Her skin was smooth and without even the slightest blemish and each part of her body seemed to have been molded and assembled with utmost precision. He did not feel like describing her legs except to point out that any man that was a leg fetish would go bananas on seeing that pair.

The more he looked at her, the more he got entrapped. He was even beginning to find it hard to talk. She on her part was as good as useless as she looked on helplessly. The fact that she was there in total nudity did not help matters either. She was pretty much the type that would be ready to enjoy life to the fullest as she looked on in her fresh nudity.

Eventually he opted for the bottle of champagne that he saw in her fridge. It was cold. As he helped himself to the drink, she went in for a quick shower. He followed suit after she had come out.

As he came out from the bath, aided by the bubbly that was already within him, he realized that she was actually irresistibly attractive. She had taken some too and she also found him the same way. They both sat there admiring each other silently. They sat there and sipped more of her bubbly till the alcohol in it was able to untie his tongue. He was the first to talk and it was to ask a question:

"Is this heaven or earth?" He asked.

"Neither." She replied.

"Why not heaven?"

"It must be limbo, maybe paradise, or even maybe none of the above. All that I am sure of is that I can no longer think logically. That is the effect that you have on me."

"I have never felt so happy and collected in my entire life and I owe it all to you."

"I am more than happy that you appreciate me."

There was no more time for words. Passion had turned them into men of action rather than those of many words. They came closer to each other with their hands trembling.

It was insane!!

It was pure madness!

It was not ones typical love story as they met in the middle of the room. They embraced and once more exploded into each other. They hurriedly tried to seek out whatever it was that they were looking for in their mouths. Passion was the driving force as they willingly and refreshingly succumbed to each other.

By the time that his hands reached her orbs once more, they were both shivering with uncontrollable passion. He had already spilled his juice and she her own. They realized what had happened and both laughed over it. Passion had never had that effect on either of them before. It was a brand new experience.

They never cared anyway. His fingers went further down to where they did not exactly belong and once more she began to moan and mutter incoherently in some unknown tongues. He did not know the meaning of all the things she said, neither did she. From the looks in her eyes, she was definitely way beyond the fifth heavens, as she threw caution to the winds. They had each gone to somewhere beyond human comprehension as they tossed and grabbed feverishly, though aimlessly, at each other.

She arched her back grotesquely. The arch seemed to have been both upwards and backwards both at the same time. It was a 'bedmatic' stance and maneuver that he had never seen before. He tenderly stroked that her center of gravity and the moan increased both in frequency, intensity and in loudness. He on his part could no longer bear it.

He then penetrated her once more. Not minding how much of in a hurry he was, it was a very gentle, steady and luxurious maneuver. He was very careful as he slowly thrust in and out. Her face immediately went into a painful but welcome and pleasurable contortion. It was a luxurious type of painless pain that she experienced. It was the type that one would never like to end. It was a sweet type of pain.

Initially he took it easy, slow and gentle, but with time his muscles began to contract and relax wildly and the thrust became more ferocious as each of them stiffened considerably in each other's arms. She shouted for him to take it easy, but immediately countered that plea by asking him not to stop and not to slow down. It was one of those paradoxes that he had failed to get his grips on when it came to such affairs.

Once more they climaxed together. Just as his hot ejaculate seared its way into the depths of her innermost caverns, hers came to meet it halfway and he felt it warm and lubricating. Each of them let out a loud cry of joy and triumph. Then came those tears of joy as she collapsed under him and into his muscular arms.

They held on to each other for a long time. They were busy muttering lots of irrelevant sweet nothings. They were still on that when sleep took over.

When they awoke, Joy was the first to open her eyes. She took a long admiring look at the hunk that was sleeping besides her and she took in all the beauty while imbibing his naked attractiveness. She looked further down and shuddered at the size, but she craved for more. She then gave him a slight kiss on his lips. Her lips hardly brushed his and she jumped up and was dressed in a hurry. It was however in a one hundred per cent see—through negligee. To make matters worse she did not put on any brassiere, neither did she put on any underpants. In other words, she had her robe on and yet she was naked. Had he been awake, he would have considered that a trap.

Her next act was to brew some coffee. It was freshly ground hazelnut flavored gourmet coffee, and it was the sweet aroma of this special brew that made him wake up. The odor had wafted tantalizingly and found its way into his nostrils and he was up in a jiffy.

She poured out two cups without a word and came to sit down by his side. She offered him one of the cups, but instead of accepting it, he did a very strange thing. He jumped up and went straight for his pants. He struggled into it as she asked:

"What do you think that you are hiding?"

"My nakedness of course."

"But I have already seen it all."

"And so what?"

"And so why try to hide it now. Don't you think that it's already too late?"

She was smiling mischievously as she talked.

"I feel helpless and vulnerable out of them."

"But you didn't feel so some moments ago. Moreover it was you who removed them to start with."

"When was that?"

"Before we did it."

"Did what?"

"Had each other."

"For dinner?"

"If you say so but please take your coffee before it gets cold."

He took the cup from her and then passed it very closely across his nostrils. That was to let that aroma waft in more closely. He made a face to show that he was satisfied with what he smelt. When it came to coffee, he knew his stuff. He was a certified coffee taster and he was also about the same when it came to women. Simply put, he knew women:

"On a scale of one to ten, I give you an eleven for this brew."

"Thanks."

"And I also give you another eleven too."

"In what?"

"As you."

"As me?"

"Yes, as you. Of all the women that I have ever set my eyes on, you are still a head above the rest."

"In what manner?"

"Be that beauty, be that intelligence, be that diligence, you are exceptional."

"Thanks for those compliments."

"Actually I didn't mean them to be compliments."

"Okay, thank you for the abuse then."

"Just the truth—the plain truth. It is the truth, the whole truth and nothing but the truth."

With that, she bent over and gave him a peck. He curdled her as he drew her closer to himself and she willingly gave herself to him just as if she had been waiting for that all her life. He realized that they were both hot on each other once more with each very eager to please each other. He however still remembered his entomology class and that made him try to restrain himself. It was all about the Drone or male bee in the bee colony. He probably knows that mating with the queen bee will be his end, but he will do that anyway. His biology teacher had insisted that the drone usually died after mating with the queen due to overexcitement and exhaustion from the act. He felt just like that and he did not want to follow that path.

"You asked me a question about getting hitched before?"

"Yes?"

"I have made up my mind."

"Please do not rush it."

He did not pay attention to her. He was already on one knee before her to pop the question that she had been waiting for all along:

"JOY, WILL YOU MARRY ME?"

He did not even finish the question before she answered excitedly. She fell on him answering yes a couple of times over and covering him with every possible smooch and hug. He was excited too as they fell on each other and rolled about in total excitement. They were both soon panting wildly as he held her particularly tightly as if he was afraid that someone else might come in and snatch her from him.

It took a couple of minutes before they could disentangle from each other, each smelling of the others sweat. Though exhausted they knew that it was time to wash up and so they headed for the bathroom for a shower. She led the way.

She let the water run hot for a few minutes as they went in before changing it to cold water. This was able to invigorate them and put them on high alert. Finally it was back to hot water. As their bodies brushed against each other in the shower, that fire was once more rekindled.

She hung on tight around his neck and was not ready to let go. He on his part put those strong biceps to use. He lifted her off the ground and she straddled him around the waist with those lovely legs. They kissed wildly as he pushed her against the wall. She did not want him to take control of all the action and so she quickly took hold of his now fully erect manhood and feverishly guided it with sure hands into her yearning catacombs. They gyrated their lower parts as each tried to out pound the other.

The water was getting too hot for comfort and so she slid him out of her and turned round to adjust the mixture of hot and cold water. He could not resist what he saw from behind as she bent over. For this reason he quickly but gingerly held her by the waist from behind. She knew what it was all about and so she bent even further. She grabbed the pipes as he once more penetrated from behind. One hand held her by the waist while with the other he went ahead to finger the frontal area. He pounded away as her now throbbing caverns joined her to pace the action, while giving it all to him.

In a matter of seconds they once more climaxed together at one and the same time. As this happened, she shouted and nearly tore off the pipe from the wall. She was however no longer strong enough to do that. He was weak too as she stood erect to face him. They looked at each other and were too weak to talk and even too weak to laugh. It was all smiles and nothing else. They were smiles of satisfaction. They turned off the water and dried up. They then raced each other to the bed, and before they knew it, each had sort of fallen asleep before the other.

It had been a tumultuous evening and it was around three in the morning when they awoke. It was her pet cockerel that called them up. He was in his cage in the corridor and it was from there that he crowed. Johnny was confused. He was sure that he heard a cockerel crow, but for it to crow from just outside their window on the tenth floor was inconceivable.

"Where did that come from?" He had asked a little bit confused.

"From my corridor."

"I thought so, but that's queer."

"No. That's Patrick."

"Patrick?"

"Yes, he is my pet cock."

It was only then that he began to relax as they laughed over the incidence.

"What's your plan now?" He asked her.

"My plan? Do you mean our plan?"

"Our plan it will be at the end, but for now it will still have to be your plan."

"What of yours?"

"My vacation has barely started so anything goes. Time is still on my side."

"As for me, I can afford to lie down here with you for ever."

"Why don't we go out and get married somewhere right away?"

This does not seem like the typical way these things happen, but it did happen. They had just met and the story is about a wedding already. That's what I call being in a hurry. Funny enough, she was all for it too.

"I would love for us to get hitched right away as you are likely to put it, but the question is where?"

"There must be a marriage registry somewhere so why don't we try to find one. Apart from that there are many independent pastors in this place and any of them could do that for us."

She was looking and concentrating on the ceiling while saying this, but finally she continued:

"I'll get the Bishop to wed us."

"That would not be a wise move at all."

"I have a very good reason for that."

"What could that reason be?"

"I have known him for about five years now, and I know that he comes from a Mafia family. If I left him for you he will definitely not be very happy and they might go after us. I can get him to officiate for us privately in the Bishops court for it. That way he will have to be silent and he will leave us alone."

"Why should that make him maintain silence?"

"You see, most people here know me as his wife. If we eloped, he will surely set his family on us. If however he officiates for us, then I will keep silent as to what had been going on. I can always claim that I divorced him, but being a man of God, he forgave me and even officiated at my wedding. I would also keep away from his wife and family. I know all of them. That way his secret will remain with him. Most importantly however is the fact that the church will not ask any questions."

"It seems as if you already have it all figured out,"

"If you however can come up with any better plan I will go with it."

"When do we go there then?"

Leave it all to me. I will call him before daybreak and make the necessary arrangements."

Joy called the Bishop as she promised and it was around five thirty in the morning. She had timed him well for that was when he just stepped into the house from a sort of all night vigil. He was expecting her to be in her room asleep when the call came through:

"Hello Mike." She said as soon as he pressed the answer button on the phone. She was the only person who called him at that number.

"Hello Joy, is that you?"

"Yes."

"Where are you calling from?"

"From somewhere across town."

"And what are you doing there?"

"Nothing right now."

"I expected that you would be at home and asleep by this time."

"I know."

"Then what's happening?"

"I have something very important to tell you."

"What could that be? Are you ill?"

"No."

"Then what is it?"

"It's about my husband."

"Your husband? But I could never have imagined that you were married."

"No, I am not married. We have been together for over ten years now and he is my husband to be."

"Your fiancée?"

"Yes."

"I never knew that you had one either."

"Well, I have always had one. And I am totally confused right now. I do not want to leave you, but he wants us to get married right away and today for that matter."

"And what is wrong with that?"

"If I do then I might find it hard to see you again."

"Why?"

"Because I will surely take my marital vows very seriously."

There was a lull as he thought of what to say again before answering:

"Are you insinuating that I am therefore a sinner?"

"No. To me a couple of extramarital indiscretions will not count as sin."

"You probably have a point there."

"I know."

"In other words, even if you got married you would not mind a couple of those too?"

"That's the point that I am trying to make. You see with women it is harder to try that."

"Who told you so?"

"No one. I just know that as a woman."

"Please my dear, don't kid yourself. I have seen more than you. I have been in a position to see and know what had been going on around. I know how many women have come to me to confess."

"That goes to show that their conscience seems to have a better hold on them."

"Not quite so. In most cases it is when they are being caught that they come for this."

He then kept quiet for a few minutes before asking:

"I have no problems with your plans, but why don't you come over for one more tryst before escaping from spinsterhood? It will have to be a sort of Spinsters party before plunging into married life."

"I would not have minded that, but the big problem is that he wants us to get married this morning."

"But why the hurry?"

"He is leaving in the evening for Baldevia. He has just been offered appointment as the chief executive office of one of the multinational conglomerates there. He was to come in with his wife and that's why it is so urgent."

"Now I can see the problem."

"If that's the case then I am very grateful to you while deeply regretting having to disappoint you."

"Oh no, you don't have to feel like that. I can never be against your progress though I will miss you."

"Thank you for being so understanding. I will always have you in my mind."

"Thanks for the time with you and may that not interfere with your marital bliss. We parsons have that saying: '*do as I say and not as I do*', so please do whatever you think is right for you."

"What an advise. That was why I had always kept myself for you."

"Thanks for that."

"One more request."

"Name it."

"Would you be willing to officiate and wed us? We could sneak into the Bishops court for a private wedding ceremony. That way a couple of things will take care of themselves. Johnny my fiancée was of the impression that I must have been seeing you. If you do officiate he would at least be convinced that it had all been church business. Apart from that, you can also be sure that our secret will remain with us. Most importantly however is the fact that we are not going to be around for people to comment. Even if they did, which is too unlikely, they would think that you are a very remarkable man. Who will believe that a man divorced his wife and then officiated in her wedding with another man if not a man of God?"

"You seem to have thought of everything."

"It is just to show how I had always appreciated you."

"Make it nine this morning in the court."

"A million thanks Mike."

With that she dropped the phone and went over to break the news to Johnny. The news was enough to make that beast inside to rear its head once more, but they were each too exhausted to pay heed to that urge. They had been drained dry too. The spirit was willing but the body was too weak to respond.

What followed is for obvious reasons left to the imagination as they faced their new lives together as husband and wife. They had become Mr. and Mrs. Cash.